Flossie Teacake

Also by Hunter Davies

Flossie Teacake's Fur Coat
Flossie Teacake Strikes Back
Flossie Teacake Wins the Lottery
Flossie Teacake's Holiday

Snotty Bumstead

Flossie Teacake

Again!

HUNTER DAVIES

Illustrated by Laurence Hutchins

A Red Fox Book

Published by Random House Children's Books
20 Vauxhall Bridge Road, London SW1V 2SA

A division of The Random House Group Ltd
London Melbourne Sydney Auckland
Johannesburg and agencies throughout the world

1 3 5 7 9 10 8 6 4 2

First published in Great Britain by
The Bodley Head Children's Books 1983
Lions paperback 1985
Red Fox edition 1994
This Red Fox edition 2000

Printed and bound in Norway by
AIT Trondheim AS

Papers used by Random House Group Ltd are natural,
recyclable products made from wood grown in sustainable forests.
The manufacturing processes conform to the
environmental regulations of the country of origins.

The Random House Group Limited Reg. No. 954009

www.randomhouse.co.uk

ISBN 0 09 996720 0

CONTENTS

1 Flossie's Hair Salon

It had been one of those long Saturday mornings and Flossie Teacake was very, very bored. She was standing in front of the living-room mirror, thinking how very bored she was.

"It's not fair," she said. "Nobody cares about me in this stupid house."

She tried out several Bored Expressions, shrugging her shoulders, sighing, rolling her eyes. Then she ran through them again. Not very good, Flossie, she said to herself. You can do better than that.

So she tried some Angry Expressions. Her big sister Bella, aged eighteen, was very good at Angry Expressions. In fact she was famous for them in the Teacake house. Everyone talked about them. And even more important, everyone took them very seriously. That was another thing that wasn't fair, thought Flossie. Bella was allowed to be angry, but when she, Little Flossie, was angry, nobody took her seriously.

And that was another, another thing. She hated being referred to as Little Flossie.

"If only I was a teenager," said Flossie to herself in the mirror, putting on one of her best scowls. "I could shout and bang doors all day long."

Flossie went into the kitchen and picked up a large pair of kitchen scissors, the red ones with serrated edges. She banged them down on the table several times, as loudly as possible, but no one paid any attention.

"Mum, I've found the scissors," said Flossie.

"That's good, dear," said her mother. "I didn't know you had lost them."

"*You* lost them," said Flossie.

"Did I, dear?"

"Oh God, everyone in this house is so stupid," said Flossie, going back to the mirror.

Her mother was clearing out the drawers of the Welsh dresser and she suggested to Flossie that Flossie might like to help, to take part in this very exciting job, to be Mummy's Little Treasure, the way she used to be when she was very little.

"Oh, no," said Flossie, groaning.

Flossie Teacake was now ten years old and was certainly not going to do any of those baby jobs.

"I'm too busy, Mum," said Flossie.

"Oh, that's good," said her mother, smiling. "I'm glad you're not bored any longer . . ."

Flossie had now changed to opening her mouth slightly so that her teeth were bared, like that scene in *Jaws*. Much better. That would frighten anyone. She gave a low moaning sound, to make it even more realistic.

"Will you shurrup, Flos," said her big brother Fergus. "You're getting on my nerves."

Fergus was sixteen and was slumped in front of the

television waiting for the football previews to come on. He was going to the match that afternoon, with his father, and maintained it was therefore *vital* for him to watch, just in case there might be any changes, new players coming in, injuries, weather forecasts.

"Well put your nerves away," said Flossie. "Then no one would stand on them. Stupid boy."

"Mum, can't you shut her up? This is important."

"All the matches are off," said Flossie. "I heard it on the radio."

Fergus just ignored her. Flossie was now waving the scissors in the mirror, pretending to cut her ears off, giving even louder groans. Fergus turned up the volume on the television set.

"Dad! It's started." Fergus went to the door and shouted upstairs. It hadn't, not quite, but it always took Father some time to come downstairs.

"I've warned you, Flossie," said Fergus, returning to his seat. "Any noise during this programme and you'll get thumped. If you've nothing to do, go up to your own room."

"I've got a lot to do, clever clogs," said Flossie. "I'm watching my hair."

"Oh, that will really keep you busy. With your horrible straggly hair. What are you doing with it anyway?"

"I'm watching it grow. So there."

Flossie did have rather thin, rather weedy hair, unlike Bella whose hair was long and thick. Her mother had promised Flossie that her hair would also be long and thick when she was older, but Flossie was not prepared to wait that long. She wanted it long and thick *now*.

She had had it cut short by a proper hair stylist a few months ago, to look like Princess Di, but now regretted it. It just seemed to stay there, doing nothing, going nowhere.

"If only my fringe would hurry up," said Flossie. "Look at it. Stupid thing."

Her fringe had actually grown quite a lot in the last month, and when she brushed it forward it was almost down to her spectacles, but she wanted it a lot longer so that she could brush it back and have a middle parting. She certainly did not want to look like the Princess of Wales any more. That style was *very* old-fashioned. Everyone in the playground said so.

Flossie put the scissors down at last and got out her hair brush and started hitting her fringe, trying to force it to grow quickly.

"Morning, Flossie," said her father, coming into the room and sitting down beside Fergus in front of the TV. "How's the hair coming along?"

"Yuck," said Flossie.

"You will keep quiet during the programme, won't you?" asked her father very nicely.

"One condition," said Flossie.

"All right then," said her father. "But gently."

Flossie ran upstairs to her father's bedroom, grabbed his brush and comb from his dressing table, and ran downstairs again. Fido, the Teacakes' dog, barked and jumped up, thinking Flossie was going to play with him. Sometimes, Flossie did try out her little artistic tricks on Fido, but only when she was unable to get a real human head to practise on.

Flossie wanted long thick hair like Bella's not just for her own vanity but to work on, a place she could treat as an adventure playground. She wanted hair she could *do* things with. She wanted enough so that she could put it into different shapes, as if she was modelling with plasticine, or try it out in different colours, as if she was using her felt pens.

In the meantime, while she impatiently waited for her own hair to grow, she was occasionally allowed, just for a few moments, if she was very good, if people were being kind to her, to brush her father's hair.

"Not too hard, Flossie," said her father. "That hurt."

"It's meant to," said Flossie. "Hairdressers are meant to hurt. It's good for the ridicules."

"Don't you mean follicules?"

But she brushed a bit more softly, not wanting her father to tell her to stop. Her father did not have a great deal of hair, but what he had was soft and gentle.

"What was it Kevin Keegan used to have?" said Flossie, watching the football programme through the strands of her father's hair.

"Two left feet," said Fergus. "He's useless."

"I mean his hair style. What was that called, Dad?"

"A perm," said Father.

"You'd look good with one of those, Dad. It would help to disguise your bald spot . . ."

After lunch, Fergus and Father went off to the football match. Bella was out all day, doing her Saturday job as a waitress.

"S'all right for them," said Flossie. "They both have things to do all day Saturday. What am I going to do?"

"Look what I've found, Flossie," said her mother. "I'd completely forgotten all about these. Goodness, they're absolutely incredible."

Flossie refused to be taken in by her mother's excitement. She wasn't going to be caught. It would just be a trick to get her to help clear out the cupboards and drawers. She knew. She went to the mirror, to have another look at her fringe. It might have grown a few centimetres over lunch. It was supposed to. Hormones or something. She'd eaten most of that horrible salad for lunch and that was supposed to have hormones. Or was it proteins? Miss Button had been explaining about them at school on Friday.

Out of the corner of her eye, watching through the mirror, Flossie could see that her mother was delving into a large plastic bag and pulling out the weirdest sorts of instruments. It looked like something from the Chamber of Horrors.

"Can I have those?" said Flossie, rushing over. "I'll try them out this afternoon on Carol Carrot. That'll teach her."

"I thought she was your friend, Flossie?"

"*Was* my friend. You don't know what she's really like. I hate Carol Carrot. I'll just tell her to put her hand in here . . ."

Flossie was holding a long metal thing with sort of spiky teeth which jumped open and closed when she pressed the back of it.

"Did they catch bears in this, Mum, in the olden days? Think I've seen one on television. Or rabbits."

"No, it was for hair, Flossie."

"Well rabbits, hares, they're all the same."

"No, silly, this is what they used for doing people's hair. Look, these are the rollers. That's a special clip for making waves or curls. Here's some special lotion."

Flossie stared in amazement as her mother proceeded to pull out of the bag more and more rollers, pins, clips, nets and other instruments, some of them in plastic and some in metal. She explained to Flossie what each was for, as far as she could remember.

"It must be over twenty years since I used them. I thought I'd thrown them all out. We used to sit for hours on a Saturday evening, our hair all covered in rollers, before we went out. We must have been mad."

She got up and went to a drawer and pulled out some old photographs of herself, with her hair all piled up on her head.

"That was a beehive, I think," said her mother, smiling at the photographs.

"Looks more like a haystack to me," said Flossie.

At two o'clock, when they had finished clearing out all the drawers, with Flossie having been a great help, without realizing it, her mother got ready to go off to work.

Mrs Teacake did not usually work on Saturday afternoons, but that day there was a special clinic. Someone was ill and Mrs Teacake had been asked to come in. She worked at the local health clinic, a medical practice with lots of different doctors, but only part-time.

When Flossie was grown up, so Mrs Teacake planned, she would go back and work there full-time. This was very unlikely, thought Flossie. The way things were going, Flossie never expected to be grown up.

"Now you will be all right at Carol's," said her mother. "You can stay for tea, but only if they ask you. Is that clear? But you're not staying the night. I need you at home."

"Yes, I heard," said Flossie. Carol *was* her best friend, when she wasn't her worst friend. She quite liked going to Carol's for the afternoon; there was always chocolate cake at her house.

Flossie stood at Carol's gate, which was only a few doors along the street, and watched her mother disappear round the corner. Then very quickly, Flossie ran home again. She put her hand through the letter-box, which she was *never* supposed to do, and let herself in.

"Carol," said Flossie on the telephone. "Flos here. Can't come this afternoon. Sorry. Yeh. Mum says I've got to stay in. Yeh. Stupid, yeh, I know. Old cow. All the same. Anyways. You what? No. Can't. 'Bye . . ."

Flossie then went upstairs to the very top of the house. She didn't go to her room. That was a very boring place. All neat and tidy and full of her school clothes and books and things. Very slowly, she pushed open Bella's bedroom door.

A notice on the door made it clear what Bella thought of *any* people who might dare to venture into her room, especially one certain person. "Keep Out, Guard Dogs, Dangerous, No Admittance and This Means You, Flossie."

Flossie opened the door, standing back carefully, in case there were any traps, and then went inside. Every time Flossie had gone into Bella's room over the last year she had been amazed. There always seemed to be even *more* things, more clothes and rubbish and ornaments and notices and busts and statues and rugs and carpets and dummies and lamps. It was like a furniture and clothing jungle, one which was growing all the time.

"Will it still be there?" said Flossie to herself. The room was very dark. Since the last time Flossie had trespassed, Bella had covered in the windows with some black curtains.

"Oh please, please," said Flossie. "It *must* be there. And it must still work. I *want* it to work."

She climbed over and through all the piles of jumble and there, in the far corner, she found the fur coat, the black and shiny fur coat, the magic fur coat, hanging up on Bella's old curly coat stand.

Very slowly, Flossie put it on. It felt even more enormous than she remembered. She almost disappeared. Only the tip of her nose could be seen, peering out. She closed her eyes and turned round several times, carefully buttoning up the three buttons, one by one, wishing as hard as she had ever done in her whole life that it would still work.

As she completed the last button, she felt a strange sensation in her body, a sort of exploding feeling. She opened her eyes—and found that the coat now fitted perfectly. She had been miraculously transformed into an eighteen-year-old, exactly the same age as her big sister Bella, the age she had always longed to be.

Flossie's body had rushed forward eight years in

time. She now did have long thick hair. Her spectacles had gone and she was tall and thin, wearing make-up and high heels, the perfect teenager.

Inside, she could feel that she was still little Flossie, with the same ten-year-old's thoughts and feelings, but outside, as far as the world could see, she was now grown up.

"Your notice in the window," said old Mrs Onions, standing at the front door. "Are you open today?"

"Of course I am," said Floz. "You silly old fool. That's why I put the notice up."

Luckily, Mrs Onions was not too good at hearing. She was peering very hard, trying to read all the words that Floz had stuck up in the front window of the Teacake house. Now she was eighteen, she was calling herself Floz. Flossie, that was just a little ten-year-old girl, someone she knew, oh, years and years ago.

Floz stepped out to admire her own handiwork. She had written the notice with her best felt pens, the ones she got at Christmas.

Speshul Today
Hair Creashuns by
Floz.
Shampooz. Setz.
Bee naves a
Speshalty.
Only £1. old
People Dun for
Half Pris.

Mrs Onions had lived in the street for many years, long before the Teacakes had arrived. She boasted that she was the oldest person in the area. Fergus maintained she was the oldest person in the world, in the universe.

She lived in a flat in the house next door to the Teacakes. She used to annoy Flossie, when she was little, by always asking her the same old question. "Do you know any poetry, Flossie?" This used to make Flossie very bored. Pop songs, yes. Jingles from television adverts, certainly. But boring old poetry. Never.

Floz had hoped that someone younger and more glamorous would have been her first customer, someone with lovely long hair, perhaps even Bella, or at least one of Bella's friends. Someone who would appreciate the finer points of Floz's hair creations.

Oh well, at least Mrs Onions would do to practise on. I'd better hurry, thought Floz. There might soon be a queue.

"Shampoo?" asked Floz, pushing Mrs Onions quickly through the front door, just in case she changed her mind.

"Is that extra?" asked Mrs Onions, taking off her shawl and hat.

"Not today," said Floz. "This is a special day. But don't tell the manager. In fact, don't tell anyone, O.K.?"

"Why ever are you wearing a fur coat?"

"Oh, well . . . my mum says . . . it's for my room-attics," stuttered Floz.

"It's funny," said Mrs Onions, "I've lived in this street for forty-two years, but I never knew we had a hairdresser's here. Right next door as well. Better than a betting shop anyway, don't you think so, dear. And better than those awful boutiques. When I came to live here the war was going on and we had no trade unions and no muggings in those days and let me tell you. . . . Ouch! Stop it! What's going on?"

While Mrs Onions had been talking away, remembering the old days, Floz had led her into the kitchen and stuck her head into the sink and turned on the tap. Floz should of course have tested it first. The water was freezing. No wonder Mrs Onions had shouted.

"Hot water? Oh, you want hot," said Floz. "We usually use cold these days, in our salons. But if you want hot, hot you shall have, my darling."

Floz had noticed that in shops and hairdressing salons, old ladies were always called "love" or "darling", especially if the person in charge was very bossy.

This time, Floz tested the water, getting it nicely warm before she put Mrs Onions' head underneath. She then opened the sink cupboard and got out a new bottle of Squeezy.

"Better take your specs off, darling," said Floz. "Don't want no soap in your eyes, do we?"

"Hmm, that's a nice smell," said Mrs Onions. "I do like getting my hair washed. The height of luxury, I always say, having your hair done. Do you mind if I smoke?"

These old women, thought Floz. They're always wanting something else.

"Sorry, love," said Floz. "My father doesn't allow anybody to smoke in here."

"Your father?"

"Er yes, that's what we call the manager. He's Italian. His real name is the Godfather. He's off today. Gone out in his gondola."

"Where's he gone?" asked Mrs Onions. "With my specs off I can't hear very well. It's true, you know. If I can see where the sound's coming from I can hear better. I was reading in the newspaper only the other day. . ."

"Here, hold this, please," said Floz rather abruptly, handing a towel to Mrs Onions. It was an ordinary kitchen tea-towel, but it was quite clean, luckily. Tea-towels in the Teacake house were often very grubby, especially after Fergus had been out playing football.

"You dry yourself while I get the things ready," said Floz.

She went back into the living room to get out her rollers and clips and other instruments.

That was the first stage in the operation safely over, or so Floz thought . . .

"Quick! What have you done to me?" Mrs Onions was shouting from the kitchen.

"Hold on, hold on," said Floz. "Oh, these customers."

"I've got worms in my hair," shouted Mrs Onions. "Look!"

"Don't say that, everyone will want them," said Floz, rushing back into the kitchen.

Mrs Onions was pulling from her hair long white strands which did look like worms. For a moment, Floz was very worried. What could have gone wrong? She hadn't started on the real work yet. Did you have worms in beehives, back in the olden days?

Very carefully, Floz pulled out one of the long worms. It slithered and slid through her fingers. She gave a little scream, then she realized what it was.

"Spaghetti, that's what it is," said Floz. "No need to worry. I told you we were an Italian hairdresser's. It's our secret ingredient. Don't tell anyone. Promise?"

The Teacakes had had spaghetti bolognaise for lunch, Fergus's favourite. It wasn't Floz's fault, but she really should have cleaned out the kitchen sink before washing Mrs Onions' hair.

"Sit over here, please," she said to Mrs Onions, leading her into the living room.

"How long have you been a hairdresser, dear?" said Mrs Onions, looking carefully at Floz, wondering where she had seen her before. There was something familiar about the face, but without her specs nothing was very clear.

"Years and years," said Floz. "I started when I was ten. I did men at first, then they ran out of hair and I had to turn to women."

"How old are you?" said Mrs Onions.

"Now, what style do you want, darling," asked Floz, ignoring the question, fluttering her eyelashes, standing on tip-toes, managing to catch a good view of herself in the mirror.

"Oh, I don't know," said Mrs Onions. "I've never been able to do anything with my hair."

"It's rather nice," said Floz, letting it fall through her fingers, the way she had seen real hair stylists do when she had had her own hair done.

"But I think you've got some split peas," said Floz.

"What? That spaghetti was bad enough," said Mrs Onions. "Dear God, what sort of place is this."

"Split ends," said Floz. "Sorry. I'll stick them together with Sellotape when we've finished. Now, how about this style?"

Floz got out the photograph of her mother taken when she was much younger, with a beehive hair style.

"I can do this," said Floz, "but it will take a long time. I might need scaffolding. Or this one over here."

Floz shoved another photograph under Mrs Onions' face for her to inspect. It was Kevin Keegan.

"Like that will do," said Mrs Onions.

"Very nice. It will really suit you. You do have very lovely hair, Mrs Onions. Has anyone ever told you?"

"It's horrible. I've got horrible hair. Just get on with it."

"I'll put some lotion on first. We always do that. The manager is very *keen* on lotions."

Floz grabbed the lotion bottle but nothing would come out. She shook it and shook it, but the contents had obviously dried up, with not being used for so many years. Suddenly, a great dollop flew out, like a large pink blancmange, all over Mrs Onions' head.

"Sorry about that," said Floz, smearing it very quickly into Mrs Onions' hair. "Terribly good for you this lotion. It's got a condition in it."

"What's this mess on my hands?" said Mrs Onions. "It's gone all pink."

"Silly old me," said Floz. "I forgot your gown. The manager will kill me for not using one. Hold on a sec."

Floz went into the kitchen and found an old apron of her mother's. She quickly put it on Mrs Onions, tying it back to front, with the buttons behind. It was rather hard to do, but it did mean that when Mrs Onions sat down again in her chair she could hardly move.

Floz then started to lay out the rollers and curlers, working very quickly and quite efficiently, remembering what her mother had told her every piece was for. One big metal clip proved very awkward to handle.

"Open your mouth, please," said Floz. Mrs Onions obediently opened her mouth. Floz then stuck in the big clip. It fitted very neatly. Mrs Onions was now hardly able to talk, as well as being hardly able to move.

Strand by strand, Floz arranged Mrs Onions' hair, then carefully rolled it up in the rollers and curlers, making it secure with pins. Very soon, she had all of Mrs Onions' hair done up in rollers. She then took the big clip from Mrs Onions' mouth and fixed it on top. Mrs Onions looked like a giant hedgehog.

"Now, I'll just get the hair dryer," said Floz. She thought that was the next stage, though she wasn't quite sure. It really was more complicated than she had expected.

"Here, these are for you," said Floz, handing Mrs Onions a pile of comics.

"Oh, that's very kind," said Mrs Onions.

"You haven't read this week's, have you?" asked Floz, giving her a Dandy and a Beano.

While Mrs Onions turned over the pages, Floz ran upstairs to her mother's bedroom. In real hairdressing salons, they had these very big hair dryers, with sort of funny things that went over your head. Floz had often seen them through the windows, long lines of ladies, sitting reading, as if they were in a space ship.

Floz brought down her mother's hair dryer, which was just a little one. Then she had an idea. She went into the kitchen and carefully wiped out the last bits of spaghetti which were still lying in the colander. That would do. Perfect.

Floz placed the colander over Mrs Onions' head, ignoring all her protests, pushing her arms away, telling her not to be such a silly.

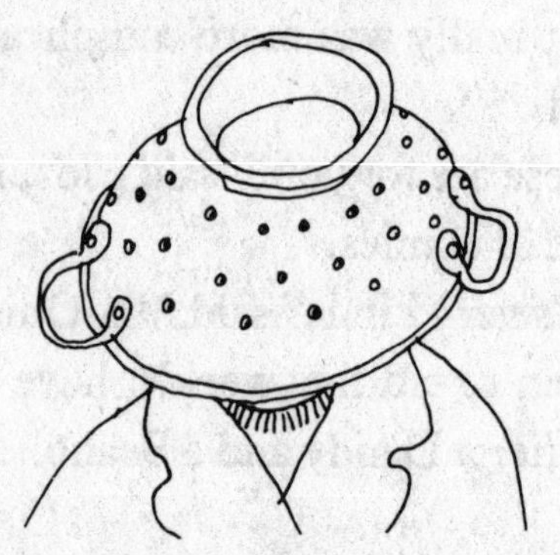

"Haven't you been to a modern hair salon before? I am surprised at you. Thought you'd been everywhere. Thought you'd done everything. Always boasting how old you are and how long you've lived here . . ."

Then Floz switched on the hair dryer and started

drying Mrs Onions' hair through the holes in the colander. It worked remarkably well. The metal sides kept the mountain of rollers in place and very soon the hair was completely dry.

"Help!" Mrs Onions suddenly shouted. "Another worm!"

"Don't panic," said Floz. "Keep your hair on." Then she burst out laughing at her own joke.

"Look, it's only another piece of our special spaghetti," said Floz. "It's nice and hot this time. Yum yum." And with that, Floz popped the piece of spaghetti into her mouth.

"Now, to finish off," said Floz, as she was taking out all the rollers and clips from Mrs Onions' hair, "I think we'll give you a spray. Hmm? We do need to set your hair."

Floz stood back to admire her good work. Perhaps she could open a full-time hairdressing salon. Even a chain of them. She could be the new Vidal Buffoon, or whatever his name was.

"Well just hurry up," said Mrs Onions. "I'm going out to Bingo tonight."

Floz went into the kitchen to see what she could use as a spray. She picked up a tin of fly spray and looked at it, trying to read the instructions, to see if it would do for hair.

"I don't want any more of that Squeezy," shouted Mrs Onions.

Floz realized that Mrs Onions was not as silly as she might look. She had better not be too cheeky, or use anything that might be dangerous. Instead, she got a can of snow spray, one they had used at Christmas time to decorate the windows with. That must be safe.

"Here, what's this?" said Mrs Onions suspiciously, as Floz began to spray her hair.

"Special Italian setting spray," said Floz. "It's our own special blend. Made from real Italians."

"It's making my eyes smart," said Mrs Onions. "Stop it."

"Yes, it makes eyes smart as well as hair smart. You look terrific."

Floz got a hand mirror and gave it to Mrs Onions so she could have a look at herself, the way they did in real salons.

Mrs Onions took a long time, studying her hair

most carefully. Her spectacles were still in the kitchen so she had to peer.

"Hmm, not bad," she said at last. "But I look a bit like a Christmas tree."

Floz had become so occupied with her work that she had not realized the time. It was almost half past four. Fergus and her father would soon be home from the football match. The living room had become rather untidy, with wet clothes and towels all over the place, the windows steamed up and the carpet covered with discarded rollers.

Floz quickly steered Mrs Onions to the front door. She did seem rather unsteady. Floz hoped she had not been too rough with her. But of course, it's not easy, if you want to look beautiful and glamorous and fashionable.

"Hairdressing is very hard work," Floz said to herself.

She was just half way through clearing up when she heard a knock at the front door.

"Oh no, they're back," said Floz. "Oh God."

Floz wiped a tiny hole in the steamed-up window

pane with her finger, then peeked through. On the doorstep she could see *three* old ladies. Floz waved at them angrily to go away.

They all stood there, hammering at the door, shouting that they too wanted a fifty-pence hair-do.

Floz quickly jumped up and tore down her home-made notice. Then she put up another one, in very large letters: "CLOSED."

Flossie came downstairs. The magic fur coat had been put back safely in Bella's room. She was Floz no longer.

She had managed to make the living room nice and tidy, well, quite nice and tidy. It had all been a bit of a rush.

Her father and Fergus came through the front door just as the first notes of the tune which introduces *Sports Report* were coming through on the radio. Fergus and Father always rushed home from the football match, just to hear the result all over again. Then at night they watched the same old stuff on the television. Flossie thought this was very stupid.

"Thanks, Flos," said Fergus.

"Yes, that was very kind of you, Flossie," said her father. "Very thoughtful."

Flossie had not just found the radio, which usually at five o'clock on a Saturday in the Teacake household was nowhere to be seen, but she had switched it on to the correct programme.

They were both very happy. Spurs, which was their team, had won. They settled down to listen to all the results, shushing each other to keep quiet.

"What's that, Flossie?" asked Father when all the reports were over.

"What?" replied Flossie.

"That notice in the window? Who put it there?"

"Oh, well," said Flossie, thinking hard, "I did it for you. I knew you wouldn't like anyone to come to the door and interrupt you when you were listening to the football results . . ."

2

Flossie Goes to the Pop Festival

Mr and Mrs Teacake had gone away for the weekend leaving Bella, aged eighteen, in charge of Fergus, aged sixteen, and Flossie, aged ten.

"You're certainly not in charge of me," said Fergus. "So get lost."

"Nor me," said Flossie. "I can do what I want. Mum said."

"Listen, madam," said Bella. "You will do exactly as I say. Otherwise you will be for it. I am in total charge of this house. Is that clear?"

"Liar, liar, pants on fire," said Flossie, skipping round the kitchen table. "I can go to bed when I like and eat what I like. Mum said. She said I had to keep an eye on *you*."

Bella grabbed Flossie by the arm and made her sit down in her seat.

"You will finish that mince, or you're going straight to bed."

"It's horrible. All lumpy. I hate it. You can't make mince, not the way Mum does. I want ice cream. *Now*. It's not fair."

"There is no ice cream," said Bella. "You eat that, or you eat nothing, then straight to bed."

"There is," shouted Flossie. "Ha ha. I've seen it." Flossie jumped up again and ran to the fridge and opened the freezing compartment to reveal three tubs of Marine Ices, chocolate, strawberry and mango. Flossie particularly loved mango.

"There you are, bossy Bella," said Flossie. "Sussed, really sussed."

This was Flossie's latest smart expression. She wasn't quite sure what "sussed" really meant, but she liked saying it whenever she thought she'd won a point. Even when she hadn't won a point, she liked saying it. She knew it annoyed both Bella and Fergus even more when she used it wrongly.

"O.K. then," said Bella. "Just eat half of the mince, then you can have your rotten ice cream. If you want to get fillings, that's not my fault, eating all that sweet rubbish."

"Ha, ha, ha," said Flossie, picking up the Marine Ices carton. "Look, real fruit flavours. Nothing artificial. Double sussed."

After supper, Bella told Flossie to clear the table. She didn't ask her politely, did not suggest that perhaps her younger sister might be kind enough to clear the table, did not even point out that the table needed clearing and it might be nice if Flossie, just for once, tried to help.

"Did you hear what I said," repeated Bella. "Get that table cleared. You."

"One word," said Flossie.

"You might help a little bit," said Fergus, looking up from reading the evening paper. He had got it all to himself, as his father was away. And he was sitting in his father's chair.

"Fat pig," said Flossie.

"Bella has made the meal," said Fergus.

"And it was horrible," said Flossie.

"Thanks," said Bella.

"And Mum did say we all had to help," said Fergus. "She wouldn't like it if she knew some of us were not doing our bit . . ."

"Two words," said Flossie. "Now you've both got to say it."

Bella and Fergus looked at each other and groaned, almost in unison. Then, this time in complete unison, they both turned to Flossie.

"*Please*, Flossie," they said together. "Please clear the table."

"That's more like it," said Flossie, triumphant. "All you have to do is ask nicely. . ."

Flossie made a very good job of clearing the table, once she had started. She very carefully stacked the dish-washer, the way her mother had told her, putting all the glasses in the right place and all the dirty knives and forks in their correct position.

"I seem to do everything in this house," sighed Flossie. "Work, work, work."

"You must be exhausted, Flossie," said Bella.

"What a treasure," said Fergus.

Flossie ignored their sarcasm.

"Miss Button was telling us about the olden days, today," said Flossie. "About when children had to work up chimneys when they were very young. Or down the mines."

"So now you know how lucky you are," said Fergus.

"Unlucky," said Flossie. "It's not fair. I'd like to go down a mine. Better than going to rotten old school. Or staying at home and being bossed around by you two . . ."

Fergus's job, after the kitchen had been cleared, was to tidy the house, picking up all the clothes and newspapers. Mr and Mrs Teacake had left only that morning, but somehow the whole house had become messed up during the day.

"People just seem to have left things lying any old where," said Bella. "Especially you, Flossie."

"Oh yes, blame me," said Flossie. "I'm going to tell on you two. You've been horrible to me."

"Good," said Fergus. "You deserve it."

"Where have they gone to, anyway? They're always going somewhere, those two. It's not fair."

"Don't be stupid, Flossie," said Bella. "They've gone to Brighton. You know that. Don't be sillier than you are. It's the first time they've been away since you were born."

"Liar," said Flossie. "What about last week?"

"That was to the pictures," said Bella. "You were in bed before they came home."

"Before *you* were born," said Fergus, "they used to go away a lot. They could leave us safely. But not you. Baby."

Flossie refused to rise to this. She knew that Fergus was simply trying to make her angry. But it did rather upset her. Not being called a baby. She didn't mind that. What upset her was any talk of a life going on in the family *before* she was born. That always seemed very strange to her.

How could anything have happened here, thought Flossie, before she was alive? The Teacakes couldn't have been the Teacakes, not without Flossie. She hated to be excluded from anything, even events that had happened long before she was born.

There were certain things she *felt* she knew about from a long time ago, the first words she said, the first toys she played with, but that was because she had been told about them so many times. They were memories of her, and so had become her memories. But events *before* her birth, Flossie found that very hard to grasp.

"Do you remember, Bella," said Fergus, "when they went away to Paris and brought us back those Eiffel Towers made of chocolate. That was really good."

"Oh shurrup," said Flossie. "I don't want to hear your boring old stories."

"And that time they brought us rock from Edinburgh . . ."

"I was alive then," said Flossie. "So. Anyway. I remember it very well. Ha ha. Sussed."

"No, you weren't," said Fergus. "I was only five. So where were you, eh?"

"I was hiding," said Flossie, deliberately knocking over all the newspapers and clothes which Fergus had just picked up.

"So there."

Mr and Mrs Teacake rang later that evening, just to see how everyone was getting on. Flossie raced to the phone, knowing it would be them, but Bella got there first.

"Yes, everything is under control. Don't worry, Mum. I'm coping well. Yes, I've done that. Yes,

Mum. Fergus will do that tomorrow. No, don't hurry back. I can manage very well. Who? Oh yes, her. Flossie. Flossie has been a *little* bit stroppy, I mean her usual self . . ."

Fergus had to hold Flossie down to stop her grabbing the phone out of Bella's hand.

"'Bye Mum," said Bella, hanging up.

"Pigs, both of you," said Flossie, absolutely furious. "I've done *all* the work in this house. I'm going to tell Mum the truth about you two. Just you wait and see. It's not fair."

Flossie threw herself on the floor and banged her feet. If only she was eighteen, the same age as Bella, or even better, if she was older than Bella, she would not have to put up with this sort of treatment. They were awful to her. All the time. Always getting at her. Just because she was the little one in the family.

"That's good, Flossie," said Bella. "Now you'll be nice and tired for bed. You are going in precisely thirty minutes. Mum said."

"Oh no, I'm not. My favourite programme's on. Dad said I could watch it."

"Dad's not here," said Bella. "I'm in charge. And because he's not here, Fergus will tuck you in tonight. I'm probably going to be out very, very, very late."

Flossie banged on the floor again, then did a hand-stand against the wall, then three cartwheels, very noisily.

"That's not fair. Why are you going out? You're supposed to be looking after me."

"You said you didn't want to be looked after," said Bella. "You said you could look after yourself. Now's your chance to prove it."

There was a loud knocking at the front door. Flossie jumped up, about to run and answer it, but Bella grabbed her arm and stopped her.

"It's probably Mrs Onions from next door," said Bella. "She'll be coming to complain about all that banging on the wall and the floor. I'll just tell her it was you, Flossie."

Flossie went back to the television. There was only another ten minutes of her programme to go. Anyway, she didn't particularly want to see or talk to Mrs Onions, not for a very long time.

She could hear Bella opening the front door, and

then the sound of her friends, other girls and boys aged eighteen, who had come to collect Bella. It was like an invasion. Flossie could hear them going "Ho ho, Ha ha," all the way up the stairs to Bella's bedroom.

Flossie went softly to the foot of the stairs and just caught the tail end, or the ends of their tails. They seemed to be all wearing long cloaks and carrying blankets and rugs. They literally swept up the stairs, their coats trailing behind them. Flossie heard a very loud bang, then a lot more laughing, as they all went into Bella's room and closed the door.

"It's not fair," said Flossie to Fido. "I hope that was one of Bella's traps. I hope it came down on Bella's own silly head. I hope it knocked her out. I hope, I hope." Flossie was trying hard to think of something truly awful to hope about them. "I hope they all fail their A levels. That's what."

Several minutes later, they all came down the stairs again, just as noisily. Flossie watched them through a crack in the living-room door. Bella was wearing what looked like a carpet. That's a relief, thought Flossie.

"'Bye-ee," said Bella, suddenly opening the living-room door and sending Flossie sprawling across the floor.

"Oh, doing more hand-stands, are we Flossie. That's a good little girl. Getting rid of our tempers, are we. 'Bye-ee."

Flossie watched her programme to the end, then she got up, smiling. She knew exactly where Bella had gone, and she also knew that Mum would not have wanted her to go out tonight, not when they were away and Bella was supposed to be in charge.

"Just wait," thought Flossie. "I'll get my own back."

She might never tell on Bella. On the other hand, it could be a useful bit of information, to be used when the right time arose.

Flossie carefully went round the living room, picking up all the clothes and newspapers which she had knocked over. She put the cushions straight, arranged her second-best felt pens and her drawing books neatly on the little table. She even cleared away a pile of orange peel which Fergus had dropped beside his chair, something which Mum really hated him doing. Then she leaned over and gave Fergus a kiss.

"Good night, Fergus," she said, ever so sweetly.

"You feeling O.K.?" said Fergus, rather taken aback. "You can stay up a bit later, Flos. If you want to. I won't tell."

"No, thank you," said Flossie. "Bella said I had to go to bed after my programme. I don't want Mum to be upset."

"Sure you're all right?"

"I'm going to bed now," said Flossie. "And there's no need to tuck me in. Is that clear? I don't *want* you to. O.K.?"

"Ugh," grunted Fergus, his eyes back on the television again.

"Right," said Flossie. "Good night, sleep tight, don't let the bugs bite."

Flossie went first of all to her own bedroom where she put a large doll and a pillow under her bedclothes, just in case Fergus did look in before he went to bed, though she was sure he would not. Fergus was far too lazy.

Then she went into Bella's room. It was even more untidy, if that was possible. All her friends had just been in, so there were lots of strange smells of perfumes and smoke. Flossie looked around for the fur coat. But it had gone.

Flossie stood in the middle of the room, completely puzzled. Bella had clearly been wearing some stupid carpet. Flossie had seen that with her own eyes. None of the other friends had on the coat, or Flossie would have noticed. But the coat stand was definitely empty. Flossie could feel tears coming into her eyes. Her little plan was not going to work.

"It's not fair. She has all the fun when Mum's away and I'm not allowed to do anything. Just because I'm ten they think they can push me around."

Then she began to wonder if perhaps it was somehow her own fault. Had she not helped in the house enough? Had she been too horrid? Perhaps she did not deserve to use the magical fur coat any longer?

Flossie had noticed in the past, when she had put on the fur coat, that it was when she was desperately and truly and honestly and longingly wishing to be eighteen that it had happened. Was there a bit of

spite in her this time? Did she just want the fur coat to get her own back on Bella?

"No, I *really* do want to be eighteen, this very minute. I know where they're all going. And I want to go with them. It's so unfair . . ."

Flossie started to cry, but very softly, not wanting Fergus to hear her. She would now have to go to bed, after all.

For a whole week she had been secretly listening to their discussions, hiding behind doors when Bella and her friends were making plans. She knew exactly how to get there, which tube was nearest, which pop groups were playing.

All that research and spying and investigation, it had now been completely wasted. She lay down on the floor, still crying, and pulled a pile of old covers and rags over herself to keep warm.

Flossie had been lying on the floor for less than an hour when a strange thing happened. Her body began to feel very funny. She opened her eyes and all was completely dark. She discovered that she had somehow crawled inside an old coat. She felt it carefully—and let out a little shout. It was the fur coat.

"Some of those stupid teenagers must have knocked it on the floor," said Flossie.

Very quickly she felt for the buttons and did them all up, one by one, wishing very, very hard that it would still work and that she would become eighteen.

She realized she was still lying on the floor, so she stood up, just as she fastened the last button. She felt her body immediately change. She opened her eyes, and once again she had become eighteen-year-old Floz.

"Hurray," said Floz, running down the stairs, but not too loudly. She knew that Fergus was still up, slumped in front of the television. She didn't want him to see her.

She found she had on a large pair of boots, thick leather ones, right up to her knees. They were very warm and cosy, but it took her some time to get used to them. They were the sort that Bella and all her friends were wearing.

"A sleeping bag," said Floz. "Oh God, I'll have to have a sleeping bag. I know Bella's taken one. But what are they?"

Fido nodded his head and licked her hands, as if he knew what a sleeping bag was. He did at least know who Floz was. Of all the inhabitants in the Teacake household, only Fido was ever able to recognize her, to know from her feel and smell that inside that eighteen-year-old body was still the same little girl he had always known. Right since he was born.

Fido knew nothing at all about things that had happened before *he* was born. But he didn't worry. That sort of thing never worries dogs.

Floz felt enormous in her boots and they seemed to make her fly through the streets. They were turned down at the top, so they flapped slightly. That was the style. All Bella's friends wore their boots like that.

She had taken her five-pound note with her, a last-minute thought. It was her Christmas present from her grandmother and she was not supposed to even look at it, never mind take it out of the house. She was saving it up for her school camp in the summer. Her parents were paying, but she had to have her own pocket money.

"Have you got anything smaller?" said the man at the tube station.

"I can take my boots off," said Floz, giving her best teenage smile.

"Don't mess me around. I can't change that."

"It's all I've got," said Floz. "That's all I had in my piggy bank."

He eventually found some change, and gave Floz her ticket. She had asked for a return. She knew she would have to be home by the morning, even though her parents would not be back from Brighton till after lunch. Fergus always slept in on Sunday. He would never hear her coming in. She hoped.

Floz sat on the tube, holding her fur coat tightly around her, trying not to catch anyone's eye. It was the first time in her life that she had been on the tube on her own. It was much easier than she had expected. All the directions were very clear.

"Grown-ups just pretend it's complicated," said Floz. "What am I saying? I am a grown-up now."

She looked at her ticket, and there was the proof. She had been given a full, adult ticket. If only she had bought a half price, child's ticket, she would have been left with much more money to buy lemonade.

There were, after all, some disadvantages in being eighteen.

The tube station Floz wanted was right at the end of the line, so there was no problem about knowing when to get off. Almost everyone was going to the Pop Festival.

Floz followed when they all rushed to get on some buses which were queuing up outside the tube station. She got on without paying. They might have been free, or Floz might have done a clever bit of pushing.

In about fifteen minutes, the bus drew up at the gates of a large country park. She could see in the distance a little lodge, which looked very cosy to Floz, like a gingerbread house, one of those in children's stories she used to read, when she was very, very young. There was only one problem. There seemed to be about ten thousand people all waiting to get past the little lodge.

"Oh God," said Floz. "It will all have finished by the time I get in."

"Don't worry, man," said a hippie figure with

very long hair standing beside her holding a guitar. "It will last all night. Maybe for ever."

"I should really be in bed," said Floz. "Daddy usually tucks me in at this time of night."

"Groovy, baby," said the hippie. "Right on."

"Oh thanks," said Floz, and immediately jumped ahead of him in the queue.

After that, several other people said "Right on", which was very kind of them, so Floz thought, actually asking her to jump the queue. Some of them wore beads and bangles and had very long hair and were quite old.

"Are you from the Sixties?" Floz asked a lady.

"Right on," said the lady, or it might have been a man, though she had a baby strapped to her back.

"Do you remember Queen Victoria?" asked Floz.

"No," said the lady. "Which group did she play in?"

Floz knew that the Sixties were very famous, but she was never quite sure *which* Sixties. It could have been the 1860's or the 1960's. She had never really listened in Miss Button's History classes.

Floz had been in the queue for almost two hours and despite queue jumping, pretending to be ill and asking people to clear a way for her, there still seemed to be nine thousand people ahead of her.

She noticed that several people seemed to be keeping places for other people. People would suddenly arrive and join the queue, saying thanks to their friends. Floz thought she would try this.

"Everyone is everyone's friend at a Pop Festival," thought Floz. "I heard Bella say that. So it must be true."

Floz walked ahead for about twenty metres, looking for a friendly face, then she pushed into the queue and said "Thank *you*" to them, very nicely. She stood there smiling for about ten minutes, before moving ahead again.

She had gained about a hundred metres when she found she had pushed in beside two very large boys in black jackets with nasty-looking badges and belts and the words Hell's Angels on their backs.

"Thanks awfully," she said to them. "Terribly kind of you."

"Out," said one of them, spitting on the ground.

"That's very rude of you," said Floz. "Very bad-mannered to spit. Miss said."

"Get moving," said the other one.

They were both well over two metres tall with big, bare muscular arms and they did look rather frightening, though Floz wasn't too worried. After all, she was now one metre sixty-eight centimetres, the same height as Bella. Little Flossie might have been frightened, but not a grown-up teenager like Floz.

"I've got some of those," said Floz, touching one of the Hell's Angels on his arm which was a mass of skulls and crossbones. "Transfers," said Floz. "I've had them for years. Don't you find they come off in the bath though?"

Floz felt herself beginning to grow even taller. For a moment she wondered if the fur coat might be playing more tricks. Then she realized she was being carried through the air.

"Very kind of you," said Floz. "It was a bit muddy in there. I have got my best boots on."

The two Hell's Angels had dumped her down right at the end of the queue, where she had begun. She could see ten thousand people stretching ahead.

"I'll just go and have a *look* at the top of the queue," thought Floz. "Just to say I've seen it anyway. I'll never get in now. If you ask me this is a Queue Festival. Not a Pop Festival . . ."

Floz heard some familiar sounds, just as she reached the top of the queue. "Ho ho ho. Ha ha ha." It was Bella and her friends. She recognized Martin. He had been coming round to the Teacakes' house for years. She had always been very fond of Martin, though naturally Bella always tried to keep him to herself, being mean.

"Hi," said Floz, going up to them. They were at that moment right at the very head of the queue, just about to get in.

Bella looked at Floz rather mystified. There was something familiar about this girl and the rather unusual fur coat she was wearing. Bella felt she had seen her somewhere before, but she wasn't quite sure where.

"Hi," said Martin, quickly pulling Floz into the queue beside them. "Long time, no see."

Martin was very kind and bought Floz's ticket for her.

"Don't worry," said Martin. "You can pay me back at school on Monday. You're in the Upper Sixth, aren't you?"

"Oh yes," said Floz. "I'm doing A levels and then B levels and even C levels this year."

"What about Street Levels and Level Crossings?" said Martin. He liked this sort of silly joke. Bella was not amused. She was now looking at Floz's boots.

"I always try to do my level best," said Floz.

"Well, you're a level-headed girl," said Martin.

"Oh shurrup, you two," said Bella. "Come on quick, we'd better hurry and get a good place."

Even with her own friends, thought Floz, Bella could be bossy. That was something she didn't expect.

Inside the park, there seemed to be millions of

people, most of them sitting on the grass. Floz had never seen such a sight in her whole life. It reminded her of a football match she had once gone to with her father and Fergus, though this crowd was even bigger. Or did it look more like the beach at Blackpool on a sunny day? She had once been there with her grandmother.

Then she decided it was like the crowds at a Royal Wedding. Everybody was having a good time, enjoying themselves, waiting expectantly, which was not always the case at football matches, not the one she had been to, or at Blackpool.

She would have liked to have flown up in the air and looked down at everyone, all the millions of ants, moving around, making little nests for themselves. She had not known that the world contained so many people.

Then she noticed in the distance, miles away, or so it seemed, a little stage. Was that all they had come to see?

As it grew darker, groups of teenagers started setting up little encampments, lighting fires, heating up soup on stoves, laying out blankets and beds for the night.

"This is better than being in Brownies," said Floz, smiling to herself. "Gosh, it's fun."

It took Bella and Martin and their group some time to find an empty patch of grass. When they did, it turned out to be all muddy and dirty. Bella said she was certainly not going to put *her* sleeping bag down first. It was a new one, which she had bought out of her Saturday earnings.

Martin's was a very special one, he said, as used by mountaineers to climb Mount Everest. It was guaranteed to keep space men warm when going to the moon backwards and to protect left-handed underwater divers swimming to Australia. Because of all that, he would prefer to keep it as clean as possible.

"Don't be stupid," said Bella.

"What sort have you got?" asked Martin.

Everyone turned to look at Floz.

"The sleeping bags were all asleep in our house," said Floz. "I didn't want to waken them up. Let sleeping bags lie, I always say."

"What is she talking about," said Bella.

"Then I was going to bring a shopping bag, but my mum has taken the best one to Brighton."

"That's funny," said Bella. "My mother has gone to Brighton for this weekend."

"It's a Mummies Convention," said Floz. "They usually have it at the British Museum. In the Egyptian Room."

Martin laughed at this. It was his sort of joke.

"I've got this horrible big sister, you see," continued Floz. "She usually takes everything that I want in our house, but I managed to get two big plastic bags. Will they do?"

Floz dug deep into the pockets of her fur coat and pulled out two large Marks and Spencer bags, the green ones, the sort you can put masses of clothes in. Floz had shoved them into her pockets as she was leaving the house.

"Perfect," said Martin. "Just what we wanted. They'll make a very good ground sheet."

He got out a large knife from his pocket and carefully split the two green bags.

"Are you in the Cubs?" said Floz. "I bet you're a Sixer."

Martin stuck the bags together with Sellotape,

making a large plastic sheet which he spread out on the ground. There was just enough space for Bella, Martin and their two other friends to put down their sleeping bags.

"I don't need a sleeping bag," said Floz, lying down beside them. "I've got my fur coat to keep me warm. Gosh, this is fun . . ."

Floz slept for only half an hour. The noise of the pop group from the stage, even though it was far away, made it hard to sleep. She was too excited anyway to sleep. She had never been out at night in the open air before. Her father had always promised to take her tenting, but he had never done so.

"Gosh, this is fun," said Floz. This was her latest smart remark. You said it in the playground, or in Miss Button's class, when things were *not* fun. That was the point of it.

You also said "Gosh, this is fun" when things *were* fun, which was a bit confusing, but it meant you could say things you really wanted to say, yet poke fun at yourself at the same time for saying it. Martin would understand, thought Floz.

She looked at Martin but he and the others were all asleep. She stared up at the sky, at all the little stars. She felt very comfortable and cosy in her thick fur coat. All around the enormous field she could see little lights, twinkling away, so that there seemed to be no difference between the earth and the sky.

"Hmm, I'm starving," said Floz to herself. Very carefully she got up, managing not to disturb the others, and went to explore.

She came to a huge queue which she thought at first must be for lemonade, by the length of it. What else could they all be queuing for? Then she discovered it was for the lavatory. One girl told her that she had been in the queue for two whole hours. Perhaps Pop Festivals were not so wonderful after all, thought Floz.

She found a smaller queue and this one was for food. Floz bought a hamburger and a Coke—and found she had to pay £4. No wonder the queue had been so small. She now had spent all of her £5.

"Gosh, this is fun," said Floz. Meaning this time it wasn't.

Then she remembered that the whole point of a Pop Festival was not the queuing but to listen to the pop groups. This was an all-night festival, with different pop groups playing in turn. She set off to reach the stage, stepping over bodies, peering into people's tents, just to see what she could see, being very nosy.

She suddenly fell flat on her face. In the dark, she had tripped over the two Hell's Angels.

They were fast asleep with a pile of empty bottles lying around them.

"They *are* good transfers," thought Floz, looking at their arms. "Very realistic. I wonder where they got them from?"

Floz leaned over one of them and tried to pull a hearts-and-flowers decoration from the front of his forehead. She pulled as hard as she could, but failed to un-stick it, so she soon got bored and walked on.

"Heh, what was that?" shouted a loud and rather angry voice behind her. The Hell's Angel was sitting up, rubbing his head.

"I think it's the Fuzz," he said, wakening up his mate.

"No, it wasn't," shouted Floz. "It was the Floz."

Floz finally managed to reach the stage, by pushing and shoving her way through to the front. She had to hold her hands over her ears because the noise was deafening. There were some people dancing, but most of them were lying on the grass, half listening to the group on the stage.

"They don't look as clean as they do on Top of the Pops," thought Floz. "They look as if they've been sleeping all night in their clothes as well."

The music stopped, some people clapped, and the lead singer came to the microphone and pointed down at Floz.

"Heh you in the fur coat, Eskimo Nell. Come up and give us a song."

This was not one of the main groups of the evening, just one of the smaller groups, filling in time till the stars played again.

Floz looked around, wondering if they really were talking to her.

"What's the matter?" said the lead singer. "Are you looking for your agent? Don't worry. We'll pay you. If you're any good."

Everyone around the stage cheered and pushed Floz forward towards some steps. She was quite keen, especially now she heard them talking about money.

"How much will it be?" she asked the singer as she got on stage.

"How much do you normally get?"

"Well," said Floz, thinking hard, "my mum gives me twenty-five pence a week, but if I clear the table after supper, I get an extra five pence . . ."

She could hear some cheering in the distance. She hadn't realized that her words were being carried round the ground. Perhaps she would get a chance to say hello to Bella and Martin. They would be surprised.

"What's your name?" said the singer.

"Floz."

"Right. Now we're Floz and the Fuzzies. What's your best number?"

Floz thought hard. She wasn't really very good on numbers. Drawing and sticking and making things, they were really her best things. Compositions, she was *quite* good at them.

"I could do the nines, but really I'm better on the eights."

"That's it, then," said the singer. "A big hand,

ladies and gentlemen, Floz and the Fuzzies will now give you The Eights!"

Everyone cheered and the group started to play. Immediately, Floz felt as if her head was exploding. The sound was like a thousand pop records, turned up high, all at once. All around her on the stage were dozens of wires and amplifiers. No wonder they all have fuzzy hair, thought Floz. She had seen in comics how your hair stood on end when you got electrocuted.

She let the group play for a few moments till her ears began slowly to clear slightly. It just seemed to be the same old pop music background. Anyone could sing along to that. So she picked up the microphone and started.

"Eight ones are eight. Eight twos are sixteen. Eight threes are twenty-four. Eight fours are thirty-two. Eight fives are fifty, I think. Six eights are . . ."

And there Floz paused. She always had to think carefully about that one. Was it fifty-eight or forty-eight? She knew it was one of those. She hoped she wouldn't get it wrong, not when Bella was listening. She would tell Mum.

All around, the crowds were shouting and clapping and demanding an encore. So Floz went through the eight times table once again, right from the beginning, but just up to eight fives. If only Miss Button would let her do that, she could be top of the class.

When she had finished, there was a tremendous cheer and a man appeared from the back of the stage and gave her some money. Floz took it quickly, jumped off the stage, and ran off quickly into the crowds.

Floz decided not to say cheerio to Bella and Martin but to get home as quickly as possible. She wondered if they had wakened up and had heard her singing over the microphone.

She went straight to the tube station and caught the first tube home. It was the first train of the morning. She had been out the whole night long. She looked out at the dawn breaking, lights going on in houses, curtains being pulled. She had never been out as late at night before, or up as early in the morning.

She began to worry that she might fall asleep on

the tube, but her head was too full of all the noises and the images of the Pop Festival.

"I'll have a few hours' sleep when I get home," she thought. "Mum and Dad won't be back till after lunch time."

She pulled her fur coat tightly round herself, digging her hands deep in her pockets. She realized she had forgotten to bring back the plastic bags.

"Bella and Martin can have them as a present. I won't be needing them again, not for a long time . . ."

Floz let herself into the house, though her arms were so tired she could hardly put her hand through the letter-box.

"Good evening, Fido," she said, giving him a pat. "I mean Good morning, Fido. It's been a hard day's night."

She went upstairs, humming that Beatles tune to herself. Now that would have been good, if *they* had been on the stage.

"My group were *quite* good," she thought. "And of course I was brilliant."

She took off the fur coat and hung it up carefully on Bella's coat stand. At once, she became little Flossie again, just ten years old.

Very slowly and quietly, she crept downstairs and went into the kitchen. Fido was most intrigued, wondering what on earth was going on. First she comes home at a very odd time, now she seems to be going out once again.

"Shush," said Flossie to Fido. "I'm just doing my jobs."

Flossie got out all the dishes and set the table for breakfast, something she had never done in her whole life before, though she had been asked to do it, many times.

"I just want to let them see that I *can* look after myself when they're away."

Then finally she went upstairs to her own bedroom. Before getting into bed, now feeling absolutely shattered, she put some money in her piggy bank. It was a five-pound note, the money she had been given on stage.

Now, no one would ever know what had happened . . .

3

Flossie Becomes a Nurse

Flossie was coming home from school with her friend Carol Carrot. They lived in the same street so they always came home together, but it meant they took twice as long. They were in different classes so one of them was always late out, doing recorder practice, netball practice, gym club, clearing up the art room, or because Miss had lost something and was keeping them in. That meant that the other one had to wait and then they were both late.

As they came out of the playground, Billy and Tommy, the two naughty boys in Flossie's class, stopped playing football and started following them.

"Ooh, look at Flossie," shouted Tommy. "Thinks she's it."

"Yeh," said Billy, "just 'cos she's got a new purple bag."

This was Flossie's latest and most treasured possession. She had bought it with her own money at a dance studio, a real dance studio, where real dancers went. She didn't really need a dancer's bag, not just for going back and forward to school, but she found it very useful all the same.

For a start, it was handy for carrying her sandwiches in. She took her own lunch to school because she hated school dinners. Then there were her rubbers. Flossie had twenty-four rubbers, each one a different shape and a different smell. Naturally, she needed a reasonably sized bag to carry them all in.

"I bet she's got purple knickers," shouted Billy, who at times was even naughtier than Tommy. They both started laughing at this, holding their sides, leaning against the wall.

"Yeh, with specs on," said Tommy.

Flossie and Carol walked on, ignoring them, talking to each other, then suddenly they both turned, as if at a given signal, and ran straight at Tommy and Billy, shouting and waving their bags. Carol was carrying a large canvas bag, with a red cross on it, rather heavy, but very useful for swinging at people, especially boys.

Tommy and Billy quickly stopped laughing and ran off down an alleyway. Despite being naughty and cheeky and very tough, or so they thought, they were both rather small and weedy. In fact most of the boys in Flossie's class were rather small and weedy.

Flossie was of course slightly plump. Nobody ever said she was fat. Only perhaps Fergus, trying to be cruel, might ever say that. Flossie was simply nicely built, for a girl of her age. Carol was even nice-lier built, for a girl of her age. Together, they were of that nice build which was very convenient for bashing up all the boys in their class.

"What you doing tonight, Flos?" said Carol.

"Dunno," said Flos. She was not allowed to say "dunno" at home: her parents had banned that word. She was also not supposed to say "S'all right" or "How do I know". This was lazy talking which signified lazy thinking. You must give proper answers and proper reasons and always speak in sentences. Miss Button was even stricter. If you ever dared to say "I dunno", you had to stand up in class till you *thought* of a proper answer.

"What you doing, Caz?" This was a shortened version of Carol. For that day anyway. Yesterday Carol had been called Carsy. Tomorrow she would probably be called Crazy.

"I dunno," said Carol, after a long pause, as if she really had a good answer.

"I dunno either," said Flossie, pausing first, as if her answer had also taken a great deal of thought.

"I dunno," said Carol, sighing. Then she gave a real pause. "Might play with my computer."

Flossie ignored this. She hadn't got a home computer and was not sure what it was. This one was really Carol's big brother's computer, but that would just start an argument, if she said so.

"Or the video. We've got a new video game. Did I tell you that, Flos?"

"Several times," said Flossie sharply. In Carol's house, they had all the good things in life. It wasn't fair. In Carol's house they had chips every day *and* tomato ketchup, as much as you liked. Mrs Teacake did not approve of chips or ketchup or video.

"Oh, I dunno," said Flossie. "I'll probably just go home and play with my stethoscope."

Flossie was swinging her bag from one shoulder to

the other, watching how her skirt flared out as she did so.

"Oooh," said Carol, rather worried. "Wotzat?"

Carol never pretended not to be jealous when she was jealous. And she never minded admitting her ignorance. This was one of the reasons Flossie liked her. When, of course, she did like her.

"It's an old one," said Flossie, offhand. "My mum brought it home from work."

"I've seen them," said Carol. "It's just a sort of Space Invader."

"Don't be stupid," said Flossie.

"What's it do then, Flos?" asked Carol.

"Lots of fings," said Flossie.

That was another thing Flossie was not supposed to do, drop her "th" sounds. But at school she spoke school language and at home she spoke home language. The nearer school you got, the nearer it was like school language and the nearer home, the nearer it was like home language. The dividing line for Flossie was the Teacakes' front gate.

"It's mainly for curing people, that's wot," said Flossie.

"Can you cure our dog?" said Carol. "It's got fleas."

"Don't be stupid. You need powders for that."

"What sort?" asked Carol.

"How do I know," said Flossie. Then she thought hard. Carol looked upon Flossie as an expert on everything to do with the medical world, thanks to her mother's job.

"Custard powders," said Flossie. "Try them when you get in. They're very good for fleas."

They were both standing in Carol Carrot's front path, Flossie and Carol both swinging their school bags. Carol was also swinging her front-door key which she wore on a long string round her neck. Flossie wished she was allowed to carry her front-door key round her neck. She also wished she lived in a block of flats. You always had someone to play with when you lived in a block of flats, even a little block like Carol's.

"I'm going on the stage, when I leave school," said Carol. "My mum knows how you get auditions. She's going to take me to one."

Carol was a very good dancer, far better than Flossie. Flossie *thought* she was a good dancer, in her head, but her body did not always do what she told it to.

"So am I," said Flossie. "I'll be tall and thin and like Bella by then. My mum said I will. She's kept all our heights since we were born."

"That's good, Flos," said Carol. "We can go together."

"But I'll probably be a brain surgeon first," said Flossie.

"So will I," said Carol. "We'll do that together as well. What do brain surgeons do, Flossie?"

"Look after brains," said Flossie.

"You mean they collect them. Like stamps?"

"Sort of," said Flossie.

"Sounds boring," said Carol.

"Or a nurse," said Flossie. "That's really my best favourite thing, what I want to do in the whole world."

"So do I," said Carol.

"You probably won't be able to," said Flossie.

Flossie was always boasting about the fact that her mother used to be a nurse. Flossie said it meant she could be one, any time she liked.

"Runs in the family," said Flossie. "In fact she

wants me to be one *now*."

"Liar, liar, pants on fire," said Carol, going up the path to her block. "You're just a show-off, Flossie Teacake. Flash Flossie, that's you. *And* you've got purple knickers. 'Cos I saw them. Ha ha ha . . . It was me that told Tommy and Billy."

Sometimes, Flossie hated Carol Carrot.

Flossie knocked at her front door and waited. There was no reply. She had been a long time coming home, mainly thanks to that stupid Carol Carrot.

"Mum," she shouted through the letter-box. She hated coming home to an empty house. Perhaps her mother had just gone round to the shops to get something for tea. "Mum, hurry up!"

Flossie was always home from school first, usually a good twenty minutes before Fergus. She loved those twenty minutes, all to herself with her mum, getting her full attention, plus of course a milk shake and a biscuit, particularly the milk shake and biscuit.

When Fergus came home, then it was his turn. A bit later came Bella, whose school was farthest away. Flossie didn't mind that. She could sit in front of the telly, perhaps have a second biscuit, while they all talked about boring old examinations.

"Now," thought Flossie, trying hard to rack her brains. "Did she tell me something this morning?"

Flossie was bad at remembering instructions, especially ones given hours and hours ago. Once she got to school, everything else went out of her mind.

She could of course have got in, by putting her hand through the secret way and finding the key on a piece of string, hanging inside, but she was not supposed to do that, unless it was an emergency. She had particularly not to do it in daylight, letting anyone who might be passing see exactly how to get into the Teacake house.

"I don't want to go in anyway," thought Flossie. "Not to an empty house."

She could go round to her Aunt Marion's, who lived in the next street, just to see if she was in. She was a social worker, but she was often in at this time in the afternoon, writing up reports.

"I might go and see Carol," thought Flossie. "Perhaps she'll let me play with her computer."

Then she remembered. Flossie hated Carol Carrot.

"I'm so sorry, darling," said Mrs Teacake, suddenly arriving at the front gate.

Flossie was sitting on the front step, still wondering what to do. She quickly put on her saddest face, trying hard to look as unhappy as possible.

"Oh, you poor deprived child," said Mrs Teacake, smiling at her. "Who stole your scone?"

This was a Scottish expression, which Flossie's grandmother was always using. Flossie thought it was a particularly stupid expression.

"Can you make me a pancake?" said Flossie, realizing she might as well make the most of her mother being late. "I'm starving."

Usually, Mrs Teacake did not cook anything for her three children coming home from school, though they could have one drink and one biscuit. Not a sweet biscuit, of course. That would spoil their supper which they all had together when their father came home. A cream cracker and cheese perhaps, or a Ryvita. But that was all.

"It was chaos this afternoon," said Mrs Teacake as she started to make the pancakes. "That new nurse is off ill. We tried the agency but they can't send anybody till tomorrow. They'll have to do without a nurse for this evening's surgery."

"And I want lots of lemon," said Flossie.

"Oh goodness, Flossie. There are no lemons left. That Bella must have finished the last one."

"Oh God, what a stupid house this is," said Flossie. "First you're late, then there's no lemons."

"I'm sorry I was late," said Mrs Teacake. "They wanted me to stay this evening, but of course I couldn't."

Mrs Teacake only worked part-time at the surgery, finishing at three every afternoon, normally coming home well in time for Flossie.

She was not in fact working as a nurse, though Flossie liked to pretend this. She was the receptionist. That was a very important job as it meant organizing all the doctors and all the patients. Flossie had been with her to the surgery several times and knew quite a bit about how it all worked.

"We'll have supper late tonight," said Mrs Teacake. "About six thirty. Do you hear, Flossie?"

"Can I have another pancake, Mum," said Flossie. "That was a bit yucky. I don't like them runny."

"We'll need some more eggs. I'll have to go round to the shop. Or you could go, dear. And get some lemons."

"Oh God, I'm exhausted. I've been working at school all day long. You're supposed to rest, when you come home. Miss Button said."

"Well just you rest then, dear. And don't say 'Oh God'."

"Resting's boring," said Flossie. "Think I'll go and play at Carol's. I'll be back for supper. 'Bye."

Mrs Teacake listened for the front door banging and then she smiled. She got two more eggs out of the fridge and made herself a pancake, with lots and lots of fresh lemon juice.

Because of Flossie's ever so slight weight problem, Mrs Teacake always tried to help Flossie, in any way she could, not to eat too much . . .

Flossie had not in fact gone out of the front door. She had only opened and banged it. She listened carefully and could hear her mother working in the kitchen.

Very quietly, Flossie went up the stairs to Bella's room. She knew she would have to work quickly. Bella might come home at any moment and catch her trespassing.

Flossie got down the fur coat, which was hanging exactly where she had put it back last time. She stroked it and closed her eyes, hoping desperately that the magic would work once again.

"I hope I haven't been too rude," thought Flossie to herself. When she had been cheeky, Flossie always knew it and she usually regretted it later.

"I *would* have gone for Mum's eggs, but they *need* me at the surgery," said Flossie, buttoning up the coat. "Someone's got to help them. Those poor doctors. And all the patients. I'm obviously just the person they need, with all my experience.

"Oh, if only I was eighteen, then I could be a nurse for ever and ever and help the whole world. I know I could do it now, but they won't let me. Stupid people. Just because I'm only ten."

She turned round and round, lost inside the fur coat. Just as she did up the top button, she felt her body being transformed. Her wish had been answered yet again.

Floz went straight into the surgery where the receptionist, the one who did evening duty, was on the telephone. That was one of the boring parts about being a receptionist, which even her mother admitted.

You had to spend most of your time on the phone, though Mrs Teacake was clever and usually managed to fill in forms, talk to the doctors, say "Next please" to the patients and even now and again read a magazine, while she was still on the phone.

Floz made sure her fur coat was only on one button, revealing her white uniform underneath. She paused at the door marked "Nurse", the little room where the nurse always worked.

"That's it," said the receptionist, putting her hand over the receiver. "Straight in. I'll send the first patient to you in a moment."

"Lucky I came," said Floz to herself. "They've obviously failed to get anyone. Well, they've now got the best nurse in the business."

Floz went round the room, examining all the shelves. They were piled high with boxes and jars, rows of ointments and medicines, pills and bandages. She opened several drawers and took out various instruments, many of which she had not seen before. Almost everything was inside a sort of plastic cover.

"Hygiene," said Flossie to herself. "Very important."

She put on a pair of plastic gloves, just to try them out, and a mask, the sort you put on when delivering babies. Or was it for operations? Floz wasn't sure.

"Can't mess around," she said at last, though she could have played for a long time with all the equipment, but of course she was working, being a grown-up, proper nurse.

She went to a roller in the corner, pulled out a fresh strip of special paper and laid it on the examining couch. She knew how to do this. Her mother had often let her do it.

"Now," said Floz. "Where's my real stethoscope . . ."

The buzzer went and Floz picked it up eagerly, more than ready for her first patient.

"It's an old woman," said the receptionist. "I'll send in her cards later. She thinks she's got an infestation but I think she's just imagining it. Could you have a look at her?"

"She's got what?" asked Floz. She didn't mind examining people, but she liked to know what for.

"Nits," said the receptionist.

"Oh, nits," said Floz. "I know all about them. All the boys in our class have had them."

"What?" said the receptionist. But Floz had hung up.

The door opened and in came Mrs Onions. Floz quickly ran behind a screen, scared she would be recognized.

Very slowly, Floz peeped out through a crack. Mrs Onions was scratching her head rather ferociously. Floz peered quickly round the screen. Mrs Onions hardly looked at her, she was still so busy scratching.

"Hurry up then, nurse, I haven't got all day. I'm off to Bingo tonight."

"What seems to be the trouble?" asked Floz.

She had often heard the doctors use this phrase. She should of course have been sitting behind a desk, half looking through some notes and half looking at the patient, taking little glances and giving little smiles. That was how real doctors did it. Nurses usually just stood waiting, checking people who came in for minor treatment or who were passed on by one of the doctors for tests. What nurses didn't do, Floz suddenly realized, was stand hidden behind a screen.

"Sorry about that, Mrs Onions," said Floz, coming out. "Just finishing important work. Very confidential. Got to be done behind the screen. Please take a seat, Mrs Onions."

"Well at least you know my name," said Mrs Onions. "I've been coming here for thirty years and they never ever know my name. Mind you, I never see the same face twice. I remember once when I came with . . ."

"Yes, quite," said Floz, grabbing Mrs Onions suddenly by the hair so that she almost jumped out of her seat.

"Stop it!" yelled Mrs Onions.

"Just testing," said Floz. "Yes, the hair still works. Can't see any breaks in it or sprains or any signs of damage."

"It's been that itchy," said Mrs Onions. "Ever since I went to this funny hairdresser place. It was very cheap, I will say that, but very peculiar. I think the young woman was foreign. The towels were filthy. So I think it must be nits."

Floz looked round for a pencil or a ruler. When she had had nits, when she was very little, the school nurse had looked in her hair with a sort of little wooden instrument.

In the corner, against the wall, Floz noticed a window pole, about three metres long with a hook on the end, which was used for opening and closing the top windows.

"Ah," said Floz, "just get my special instrument. Won't be a tick. This will soon frighten off any nits."

Floz grabbed the pole and started poking it around inside Mrs Onions' hair.

"I don't know about the nits, but you're certainly frightening me," said Mrs Onions.

Floz laughed, the way nurses do when patients are being rather silly and tiresome.

"Ouch!" shouted Mrs Onions. "That hurts."

"Well, you want to be better, don't you?"

There was a knock at the door and Floz turned round, still holding the pole. As she did so, she knocked everything off the shelf behind her and all the ointments and jars fell with a clatter.

Floz bent down to pick them up, and this time the pole sent Mrs Onions sprawling from her chair. Floz was helping her up when the door started to open. Floz moved towards it but the pole, which she was holding in front of her, immediately slammed the door shut. There was a loud yell from the other side. It sounded like one of the doctors.

"Can't you just give me some medicine?" said Mrs Onions. "That's what they used to give in the old days. Sort of purple stuff. You rubbed it on the scalp."

"Purple stuff," sniffed Floz, trying to be superior, at the same time looking round the room. "That's *very* old-fashioned. These days we use a much more modern system. It's called Blue Stuff."

With that, Floz poked her finger in a bottle of ink and dabbed a large blue patch on Mrs Onions' grey hair. It looked as if she had been given a blue rinse.

Floz then pushed her to the door, opening it first to make sure none of the doctors were around, and shoved her out.

"Next please," said Floz, talking into the phone.

Floz went to the wash basin in the corner to wash her hands the way good nurses should after every patient, and looked up to see that Miss Button was standing in front of her.

"Oh Miss," said Floz. "Er, I want to leave the room now . . ."

"What?" said Miss Button. "I was told you would take my blood pressure. You are the nurse, aren't you?"

"Oh yes, of course I am. Sorry about that. I've had such a tiring afternoon. So many silly people."

"I think I'm just really run down, doing too much. I'm a teacher you see, a class of ten-year-olds, and they're very exhausting, especially some of them . . ."

"I quite understand," said Floz. "Open up, please."

"Open what?"

"Well your purse, if you like. I've spent all my pocket money this week."

"What?" said Miss Button.

"Just a joke," said Floz.

"You're supposed to be testing my blood pressure."

"Bloody pressure," said Floz. "There's no need to swear."

"I didn't swear," said Miss Button, starting to lose her temper. "You did."

"Yes, I can see you are overworked. We always test people with jokes first. Why don't you have a holiday? A very long one."

"I've just had one," said Miss Button.

"I forgot," said Floz. "Teachers have long holidays all the time."

Floz went across and forcibly opened Miss Button's mouth.

"Hmm, just as I thought," said Floz, looking deep inside. "You've strained the blue tonsils, that's why you're getting bloody pressure. You must stop shouting at the children. That's the only cure. Now, you will do as I say, won't you? Especially the girls in your class. You mustn't shout at them any more."

"This is really all most peculiar," said Miss Button.

"Tongue out," said Floz.

Very slowly, Miss Button did as she was told.

"Hmm," said Floz. "Now you're being rude again."

Miss Button turned to go, but Floz grabbed her by the hand.

"Breathe in deeply," said Floz, holding Miss Button's hand. "This is the final test. It won't hurt."

Floz put her hand in the pocket of her fur coat and pulled out a Mickey Mouse watch, one of those pretend ones, but she put it to her ears quickly, so that Miss Button could not quite see it.

"Yes, fine," said Floz, listening to it carefully. She knew there was some test you did using a watch, but she wasn't quite sure which one. "Yes, blood normal, skin normal, bones normal, shoes normal. Just be careful about the shouting."

"Is that all?" said Miss Button, rather wearily.

"Yes, you will be quite all right, Miss Button. No need to see the doctor. Next patient, please."

Four people then entered the room, to Floz's surprise: two rather bossy-looking ladies with very hefty arms and serious looks on their faces and two little boys of about ten, each of them cowering behind their mothers. It was Tommy and Billy.

"They've had an accident, you see," said one of the mothers.

"They got chased by these two big bullies," said the other mother. "Huge girls they were. They chased these poor little boys down a cobbled alley and they fell. The doctor says nothing's broke, but he says you'll have to dress their wounds."

"Well first of all," said Floz, "I would like you two ladies to wait outside. If you don't mind. Nurses' rules. If you don't mind. Thank you."

Then she ushered them both out. She stood before Tommy and Billy, drawing herself up to her full one metre and sixty-eight centimetres. "*Show* me the wounds," she commanded.

Very slowly, they rolled up their trousers to reveal a few small cuts.

"Wounds!" said Floz. "Baby scratches. What cry-babies you two boys must be."

"It was me mum," said Tommy. "I didn't wanna come."

"It was me dad," said Billy. "He said he wouldn't write no more notes to get me off school. He said I'd have to have a doctor's note."

"Well, first of all it will mean a blood test," said Floz. "Very important in these cases. You never know, you might go round biting dogs. You could give them a doze of rabits. One can't be too careful."

Floz got a little syringe from a drawer wrapped in a neat plastic cover. She'd once had about twenty used syringes at home, old ones which her mother had brought home for her to play with. They were very good for water pistol fights.

Floz unwrapped the syringe and held it under Tommy's nose, so he could see the very sharp point.

"This won't hurt at all," said Floz brightly. "No more than a leg falling off or being run over by a bus. You'd better watch this, Billy. *You* will be next."

They were both shaking with terror, but Floz held them firmly, one in each hand.

"Now let me see, your arms are rather scrawny. It will have to be your bottom. I bet you've both got fat bottoms. Trousers down, please."

They both looked at each other. Tommy asked if he could get his mother. Billy said his father had told him never to take his trousers off.

"You *are* old enough to take your trousers down by yourselves, aren't you? Good gracious. Ten years old. You'll be telling me you can't tie up your laces next. Right, if you want *me* to do them for you . . .

Very slowly, Tommy and Billy both pulled down

their trousers, carefully holding their shirts in place.

Floz gave them a very quick jab each. It was just a pretend jab, with her finger, but they both let out a huge yell as if they were being tortured.

"Very interesting," said Floz. "Purple underpants, I see. From Marks and Spencer's. Very fashionable."

She dabbed some TCP on their bottoms and put a large piece of Elastoplast on their legs. In the bottom of a drawer she found some old Smarties and gave them two each.

"That's for being brave little soldiers," said Floz. "Next time, don't run after girls and shout names at them . . ."

When Tommy and Billy had left the room, Floz picked up the phone and told the receptionist not to send anyone else in.

It was now six o'clock, the official closing time for the surgery, though there were still a few people sitting in the waiting room. Floz knew she would have to hurry home or she might be late for supper.

" 'Bye," she said to the receptionist, rushing out of

the surgery. "Got to dash. I've got a big operation at the hospital. Brain surgery . . ."

Floz ran all the way home and managed to get into the house and upstairs without being noticed. She took off the fur coat and hung it up safely in Bella's room.

"Sorry I'm late," said Flossie, sitting down at the kitchen table. All the Teacakes were already assembled, though the meal had not yet begun.

"What's that funny smell?" said her father.

"Hmm," said Bella. "It's like TCP."

"What have you been doing, Flossie?" asked Mother.

"You know," said Flossie, "I've been at Carol's. She wanted to play Nurses."

"You're not still playing those baby games, are you?" said Bella.

"That's right," said Flossie. "Well, I am a baby. I'll probably never grow up . . ."

4
Flossie Goes Baby-Sitting

The Teacakes were entertaining. Mr Teacake thought they were always entertaining, especially when he was talking and telling stories. Mr Teacake was very fond of his own stories. Flossie was not sure.

On this occasion, the Teacakes were entertaining their relations from the country to Sunday lunch. Flossie always enjoyed their visits because she could play with her cousins, Ross and Lindsey, who were around her age. Flossie was in fact the oldest, by eleven months, two weeks and thirteen hours, but she very kindly allowed Ross and Lindsey to think they were *almost* as old as she was.

"Let's go to your room, Flossie," said Ross.

"Yes, let's," said Lindsey. "Then we can dress up."

Flossie really preferred to stay downstairs, even though it had become very noisy with people drinking glasses of wine and eating silly little biscuits and nasty green-looking dips and shouting at each other and not listening.

"We might miss something," said Flossie.

"What?" said Lindsey.

"Some secrets," said Flossie.

"You mean sweets," said Lindsey. Lindsey was very fond of sweets. "Will they be giving out sweets if we go away?"

"Probably," said Flossie. "They're always horrible like that."

"Then I'll stay," said Lindsey.

"Come on, Flos," said Ross. "Let's go to your room then."

When Flossie was visiting her friends' houses, she always loved to go to their rooms, even when they didn't have rooms of their own, even if they shared with their brothers and sisters. If she went to Ross's house in the country, far away in Bedfordshire, she always liked to poke around his bedroom, look at his toys, his clothes, his games and his books.

"I want to stay downstairs," said Flossie.

"Oh, go on," said Ross.

"My room is so boring," said Flossie. "I hate my room. I know everything in it and it's vee boring."

Saying "vee" instead of "very" was the latest smart thing in Flossie's playground.

"What's vee boring, Flossie?" asked Ross.

"My room is," said Flossie. "So are you, for wanting to see it."

Ross gave her a friendly push, just friendly enough for her to fall over and land in a plate of crisps which happened to be lying on the floor. Then she pulled Ross on to the floor to fight, only a friendly fight, but they happened to roll over just as Mr Teacake was placing a glass of red wine carefully on a little table beside his chair.

"You stupid fools," shouted Mr Teacake as the glass of wine fell over. Then he realized they had company. The Teacakes were entertaining and the Teacakes should not be seen to shout and be so angry. Especially Mr Teacake.

"Do be a little more careful, children," said Mr Teacake, smiling. "Why don't you two go upstairs and play, hmmm?"

"Come on," said Flossie, sighing. "Let's go. Who wants to stay with these boring people anyway."

Ross started a careful inspection of Flossie's room, as if he was an army sergeant doing a kit inspection.

Flossie's room was particularly tidy as Flossie had recently been doing it. Her mother had said that on no account was she going to let Flossie's room get like Bella's room. One dump was more than enough. Flossie thought this was very unfair.

"Look at this," said Ross. "This glass animal's broken. Why don't you mend it with Super Glue?"

Flossie lay on her bed, pretending to be half asleep, staring at the ceiling, humming to herself. Not a tune. Just a non-tune, knowing it was annoying. Mr Teacake always found it very annoying when Flossie started humming her non-tunes.

"You shouldn't use drawing pins on the walls, Flossie," said Ross. "You should use Blu-Tack."

Flossie made no reply.

"This photograph is torn. Why don't you stick it with Sellotape, Flossie?"

"Why don't you get lost, Ross."

"I've got one of those," said Ross, continuing round the room.

He was pointing to a certificate for gym which Flossie had pinned on the wall, Grade Four, BAGA Award.

"Oh, that old thing," said Flossie. "That was ages ago."

"Only mine is Grade Two," said Ross. "I'm doing Grade One next week."

"How boring," said Flossie.

"And I've got all *those* swimming badges," said Ross. "Haven't you done your mile badge yet? Only one hundred metres. Huh. I did that in the Infants."

Flossie was determined to ignore his showing off. Ross was now looking at a certificate Flossie had won for being runner-up in a drawing competition.

"This looks good, Flos. Didn't know you'd won this. You didn't have it last time I came. How many entered?"

Flos was not quite sure. It might have been twenty. It happened when her class was at the local children's library for a lesson. Not all of them had entered. Perhaps it was only ten.

"Millions," said Flossie. "It was the whole of London. So that must be millions. Not like stupid old Bedfordshire. Nobody lives there. Easy to win things like mile awards, living in stupid old Bedfordshire . . ."

Ross jumped upon her and they both rolled on to the floor.

Flossie enjoyed teasing Ross. She knew he could take teasing, not like some people she could mention, such as Carol Carrot.

It did mean, however, that Flossie's very tidy room very soon became very untidy, even vee untidy, with clothes and ornaments scattered everywhere as they rolled all over the floor.

"That's better," said Flossie. "That's what a room should look like . . ."

"Shouldn't we go down, now?" said Ross. "I'm starving. It must be lunch time."

"It's always late on Sundays. We have to wait till that stupid Fergus comes back from football, and then horrible Bella comes back from seeing her horrible boyfriend."

"Wish I had an older brother and sister," said Ross. "You're so lucky."

"Me!" said Flossie. "No, I'm not. They have all the fun. They can go anywhere and do anything. I can't even have my room the way I want it."

"I think your room's nice, Flossie."

"Oh shurrup, Ross."

"Why should I. I'm not a shop."

"Ha, ha, only I forgot to laugh," said Flossie. "That's ancient. I used to say that joke years ago."

"You're so lucky," said Ross. "Living in London."

"Oh yes," said Flossie. She hated anyone calling her lucky.

"You know everything, Flossie Teacake."

Flossie was not quite sure if this time Ross was teasing her.

"Lucky beggar," said Ross, giggling.

She hit him and they started fighting once again.

"Do you want to know a secret, Ross," said Flossie.

"Is it about sweets? I'm not supposed to have them any more. I've got three fillings."

"Don't be stupid. This is a *real* secret. Something I've never told anyone, not in the whole world. It's a magic secret. Something you won't believe. Something absolutely amazing. You've never seen such a thing before."

"It *is* about sweets," said Ross.

"O.K., I won't tell you, if you're going to be so silly."

"No, please, Flos. Go on. I won't mess about."

"Well, we'll have to go into Bella's room."

Ross's face lit up. It always did, when he was happy. His whole face opened so wide and his eyes became so huge that it did look as if a bonfire had been started inside his head. Ross was always a good person to tell anything to.

"Do you think we ought to, Flossie?" said Ross.

Ross was very law-abiding. Despite all the times he had been to the Teacake house, he had never once been inside Bella's room. Flossie had told him stories about it and he had often read the notice on the door.

Flossie and Ross stood at Bella's door, listening carefully. Ross's lips were going, not through terror or even excitement. He was reading the notice. His lips always moved when he read anything.

"Keep Out, Guard Dogs, Dangerous, No Admittance and This Means You, Flossie. AND YOU ROSS."

"That's typical of her," said Flossie. "Just 'cos she knew you were coming today. Just ignore it. I always do . . ."

And with that, Flossie pushed Bella's door open.

Ross could hardly believe his eyes, large though they were. He had been told by Flossie that Bella's room was untidy, but he never expected it to be this untidy.

"Cor," he said. "It's like a jungle. Hope there's no lions in here . . ."

"Lots, all of them hiding, so be careful," said Flossie. "And don't move anything around. Bella has traps all over the place."

Ross suddenly grabbed Flossie's hand. He had seen what he thought was a bloody head, lying on the floor, amidst a pile of arms and legs.

"They're just dummies," said Flossie. "Dum dum."

Then Ross walked into a skeleton which was hanging from the ceiling and he let out a scream.

Flossie stopped and listened, worried that someone would hear they were in Bella's room. She put her hand over Ross's mouth, just in case he made any more noise. He screamed even louder, thinking one of the dummies had come to life.

Eventually, Ross grew a little braver. His eyes got used to the darkness and he could see that every surface, every wall, and the ceiling and floor, was simply being used by Bella as a display area for her hundreds of possessions.

"How can she find anything?" said Ross. "It's like a bull in a jumble sale."

"China shop, stupid," said Flossie.

"O.K., a china shop in a bull."

"Just try to climb over things very carefully," said Flossie.

"Ooh, what a pong," said Ross.

"It's these old clothes. She gets them from skips and jumbles and never washes them. Mum refuses to come in here any more."

"Don't blame her. All Bella's clothes are scruffy."

"Not all of them," said Flossie.

"Oh yes, they are," said Ross.

"Then look at this then!"

Flossie had been leading Ross by the hand, over various mountains of clothes, down valleys of ornaments, through tunnels of carpets and blankets, and was now pointing to the fur coat, hanging on the curly coat stand, where she had last left it.

"Ugh, horrible," said Ross. "Bet it's full of fleas. I wouldn't wear that for anything."

Flossie considered whether they should leave Bella's room at once. Perhaps Ross was not quite the right person to impart her secret to. Perhaps she had made a big mistake by bringing him into Bella's room in the first place. Perhaps he would now ruin everything . . .

"What would you do if you were eighteen?" said Flossie.

"I dunno," said Ross. "What would you do?"

"Lots of things," said Flossie. "I've done many of them already."

"What a liar," said Ross. "Flossie Teacake, you're a big liar."

"I just want to be eighteen," said Flossie, "grown up, like Bella, not bossed around, treated as a baby, told off, not allowed to do things, not allowed to go anywhere, not allowed to have my room as I like it, oh if only I could . . ."

"I wouldn't mind playing at Wembley," said Ross, after a lot of thought.

"For Spurs," said Flossie. Spurs were Fergus's team.

"Not that rubbish," said Ross. "For a good team. Man United. That would be magic."

"Magic can come true," said Flossie.

"I'd like to walk out at Wembley with the crowd cheering and all that. For Man United. That would be really good. They'd all be shouting 'Come on Ro-oss, Come on Ro-oss.' I'd need a longer name, though, something longer than Ross. Trevor, or Kevin."

"When you're eighteen," said Flossie, "you can change your name to anything you like. You needn't be Ross any more, not when you're eighteen. I'm always Floz, when I'm eighteen."

"Don't be stupid," said Ross. "You've never been eighteen. You're just pretending."

"Do you see this fur coat, Ross?" said Flossie, half whispering. "Promise you won't tell anyone."

"Yeh, magic," said Ross, looking round, nervously. "Let's go. I don't like this room. It's sort of eerie."

"All you have to do is put it on, close your eyes, wish you were eighteen and able to do something that an eighteen-year-old does, then you turn round three times, still wishing, and slowly button up the three buttons. Then it happens, the magic starts working and you turn into . . ."

Flossie was speaking quietly and softly, trying to get Ross in the right mood, feeling rather strange herself, her skin slightly prickling.

"Come on, Ross. Put it on. Then you'll be ready to walk out at Wembley."

"I think I'd be scared to play at Wembley. What if I score an own goal . . ."

"Not if you really are eighteen. If you really *want* it to happen enough, then it will. Come on. Just try it on once."

Very slowly, Flossie helped Ross on with the coat.

Ross had completely disappeared from sight. He was lost somewhere inside the depths of the coat, just as Flossie usually was when she first put it on. She could hear Ross grunting as he stumbled around inside.

"It's such a beautiful coat," said Flossie, feeling its black smooth surface, rubbing her nose against the collar.

"I'm lost," said Ross. "Put the light on. I want out."

"Just close your eyes, Ross, and wish very hard."

Ross was moaning and mumbling, saying that he was starving, he was cold, he was choking, he wanted the lavatory, he wanted his father, the coat was stupid and anyway he didn't want to go to Wembley. Then there was silence.

"Are you all right, Ross?" asked Flossie, worried in case he had suffocated.

Then very slowly the coat started turning round. Ross's little fingers crept out and began buttoning up the buttons, one, two, three.

Flossie stood for a moment, holding her breath, scared to move or talk. Then she almost pounced upon Ross, desperate to see if he was now ready for Wembley.

Nothing had happened. Ross was still crouching inside the coat, still as small, still a nine-year-old boy, still muttering and mumbling.

"I told you it was stupid," said Ross. "I knew you'd just made it up."

He jumped over the piles of clothes and made for the door, followed very slowly by Flossie.

"Have I ruined it now," thought Flossie, "for ever and ever? I should never have told anyone my secret . . ."

It was chicken for lunch, which Flossie loved, and French beans, which she also loved, and then chocolate pudding afterwards. Because there were visitors, there was also lemonade, all the way through. Flossie did enjoy her relations coming to lunch. Except for Ross. Ross was no longer her favourite cousin.

"I want a year off," said Bella, stuffing herself. "After A levels. I don't want to go to college right away. I want a year off doing something interesting."

All the adults then started discussing examinations and which college or university Bella should apply to and what they had wanted to do, or tried to do, or failed to do, when they were eighteen.

As far as Flossie was concerned, it was all vee boring. She gave Ross a few kicks under the table, just to annoy him, but he was too busy having seconds of chicken to notice.

"I want a year off, too," said Flossie. "When I leave primary school. Before I go to Bella's school."

"Don't be silly," said Mr Teacake. "You don't have a year off when you're only ten. You stay at school all the time, till you're eighteen."

"I want to be eighteen now," said Flossie.

"Yes, dear," said Mr Teacake. "You've told us. So do we all."

The adults laughed at this and Mr Teacake was pleased and handed round some more wine.

"It's not fair," said Flossie.

But by this time, nobody was listening to Flossie. They were now discussing the evening's arrangements. Ross and Lindsey and their parents were all going to stay the night nearby at Aunt Marion's house.

"You're still free, are you, Bella?" said Lindsey's father.

"Oh God," said Bella. "I forgot to tell you. I've got

tickets for a gig. I didn't think I'd get them, but I did. So I can't baby-sit after all. Sorry."

All the adults in the Teacake family were going out that evening, and had hoped that Bella would baby-sit for Ross and Lindsey.

"Tell you what, though," said Bella. "As it's my fault I'll definitely get someone for you. We're not all going to the gig. Martin hasn't got tickets. I'm sure he'll baby-sit. Anyway, somebody will. Don't worry."

"That's good," said Mr Teacake. "More wine anyone?"

He had given every adult three glasses so far. Flossie had been counting. That was not like him. He was usually very mean with drinks, of all sorts. He must be entertaining today, thought Flossie.

Mr and Mrs Teacake left home about seven o'clock that evening. Mrs Teacake told Flossie to be very good and instructed Fergus to make sure Flossie was in bed by eight o'clock.

"Oh no," said Flossie.

"All right, half past eight, but no later," said Mrs Teacake.

As soon as they had gone, Flossie told Fergus that she was feeling tired and was going to bed now. She would read for a bit, as she had a very good book to read, a funny one about a naughty ten-year-old.

"No need to tuck me in," said Flossie. "In fact I don't want *you* coming into my room. I'm going to put up a notice on my door, just like Bella."

Fergus didn't reply. He was slumped in front of the television, a book about the history of the Second World War on his knee, the one he was supposed to be reading for his O levels.

"I'm telling on you," Flossie said. "You're supposed to be doing your homework."

Fergus didn't reply.

"O.K., I won't tell," said Flossie, "not this time, if you're nice to me . . ."

She then went upstairs to Bella's room. Nothing seemed to have been altered. Bella had been in the room in the afternoon, but not for long, rushing off early to her pop concert.

"Will it still work?" said Flossie to herself, going carefully across the room. "I hope that Ross hasn't ruined everything. I shouldn't have let him try it on. Stupid boy. I shouldn't have told him anything about it. I'll never ever tell anyone again. That's if it works. Oh, I do hope it works . . ."

Flossie put the fur coat on very quickly, then very quickly took it off again. She didn't want to rush things. She wanted to go through every movement, every action, exactly as she had done that very first time. She knew she would have to wish very hard, far harder than she had ever wished before, to make the magic start working again.

Flossie closed her eyes and very carefully buttoned up the coat, wishing and wishing to herself. She kept her eyes closed for a long time, scared to open them and perhaps find that nothing had happened. She did feel a bit funny, but that could have been excitement. Or fear.

If it didn't work this time, would anyone ever believe that once, when she was just ten years old, she had changed by magic into her own self, eight years ahead, rushing through time and space and landing in the body of Floz, aged eighteen?

It worked!

"Bella sent me," said Floz, as Ross's father opened the door. "I'm your baby-sitter."

"Oh, you're early. Didn't expect you till a bit later."

"I like to be early," said Floz. "I'm always early for all my baby-sitting jobs."

"That's good. Actually, I thought a boy was coming. Someone called Michael?"

"Martin," said Floz. "Couldn't make it. He asked me instead. I'm much better anyway. I have a way with children. I have been a nurse as well, though I don't usually talk about it."

"Well, I'll show you where they are. They're both asleep, luckily."

"I know my way around, thanks," said Floz. "I mean, I know my way around children."

Floz was taken in to the bedroom where Ross and Lindsey were fast asleep. At least they looked fast asleep. Floz thought she detected a slight flicker in Ross's right eye, but she could have imagined it. She hoped.

"Help yourself to anything in the fridge," shouted Ross's father from the front door.

"Thanks," said Floz. At that moment, she was

already looking inside the fridge.

"The rotten lot. Just a load of rubbish. Old cucumbers and bits of stale cheese. Typical of Auntie Marion. Not fair. When Bella does baby-sitting, she always gets left chocolate cake and cheese cake and biscuits and lots of drinks. I'll be putting this place on the Black List."

Bella and her friends all had a baby-sitting Black List. Your name went on this if you offended Bella and her friends in some way. For example, you might not leave out enough food. Or you might leave the children awake and they had to be fed and put to bed. Or they woke up. Or the parents did not come back at the time they said they would. Or when they paid you, they didn't give some extra money. That was the worst crime of all. According to Bella and her friends.

"I don't care if I get paid or not," thought Floz, munching a piece of stale cucumber.

She had managed to find some salad cream and some not too stale cheese. On another shelf she had discovered, hidden away, a tin of tuna fish, two tins of sardines, some beans and some tomato ketchup, all of which she had mixed up together on a large plate.

"When you're a teenager," said Floz, "this is the stuff you eat, all the time. I've seen Bella do this—in between her proper meals."

She listened carefully. Had she heard Ross getting up? No, it was just her imagination.

"Ugh," said Floz, starting to eat the mess on her plate. "I feel sick . . ."

There was silence for the next half hour. Floz sat and watched television and gradually her sickness receded.

She then went into the bedroom to check that Ross was asleep, which he was. She got the disgusting plate of food, the one she had made for herself, and put it under Ross's bed. They would now think it was Ross's fault. Serve him right. The pig.

There was a sudden knock at the front door. Could that be the parents, coming home early? Floz looked through the blind and saw that it was Martin, looking rather hot and worried.

"I'm in charge," said Floz, opening the door.

"Oh hi," said Martin. "Sorry I'm late. Got held up. I've come to baby-sit."

"Too late, buster," said Floz. "You were late, so they got me. Paying me double, and all the food I can eat and drink. Come in anyway. Have some champagne."

Martin came in and Floz searched through the cupboards. She had just made it up about champagne, but she had seen a few bottles on the shelves. When you're eighteen, you're allowed to drink anything you like. After all, she had been told to help herself.

"Do you like cherry brandy, made out of real cherries?" said Floz, looking down a row of bottles, most of them empty. "Or port, made out of real ships? Or some vodka?"

Floz held a bottle up to the light. "It's just water. What a swiz. I know, what about something called Guinnless? There's a bottle of it here. It looks black and yucky."

Floz gave it a good shake, to make sure there was something inside, then opened it. The drink flew all over the room, covering Martin most of all.

"Ugh horrible," said Floz, taking a sip. "Let's try this whisky. Got a nice picture on the front. Here, Martin, you can finish it. No no, go on. We'll have our own party. That's what baby-sitters often do."

They sampled a few more bottles, then Martin said he didn't want any more. He had had enough. And with that, he fell asleep.

"Oh no," said Floz. "Now I've got *three* babies to look after. And I feel even sicker . . ."

About eleven o'clock, Floz decided to go in and look at Ross and Lindsey. She had heard this awful noise, like a herd of pigs, being driven to market. She had checked it wasn't Martin. Perhaps it was mice.

Ross was still asleep, but with his mouth wide open, snoring so noisily the whole bed was shaking.

"He is a pig," said Floz. "Shurrup, Ross. I can't watch telly with all that noise."

Ross carried on snoring so Floz went back to the kitchen and got a clothes peg which she fastened on Ross's nose. It fitted very neatly. She'd read about this in a children's book—called *Little Women* or *Little Girls* or something. Immediately the snoring stopped, so Floz went back to the TV.

From the bedroom came the sound of an enormous "Ping"! Floz thought for a moment Ross might have exploded.

"I've had a nightmare," said Ross, sitting up in bed, looking around, blinking his eyes.

"You are a nightmare," said Floz, rushing in.

"I dreamt someone drove a car into my mouth," said Ross.

"Well it's big enough," said Floz. "It's about the size of the tunnel at Wembley Stadium. Not that *you've* ever been to Wembley. I can see you're too silly to want to go anywhere interesting or exciting like Wembley . . ."

"Who are you?" asked Ross.

Floz thought hard. For a moment, she almost blurted out the truth, but she had vowed never again to tell anyone in the whole world her secret.

"You wouldn't believe it, even if I told you," said Floz. "I'm sometimes the Queen of England, but tonight, I'm your baby-sitter. And if you are not asleep in two minutes, I'm going to spank your bare bottom."

"Don't you touch Rossy," said Lindsey, waking up, "or I'll scream and I'll scream and I'll scream."

"Oh God," said Floz. "Now both of them are awake. You will both definitely go on my Black List."

"Don't you say 'Oh God'," said Ross. "My grandmother doesn't let people say 'Oh God'."

"Shurrup!" shouted Floz. "Both of you."

Ross and Lindsey got out of bed and started shouting back at Floz, saying they wanted their mum and dad, at once.

"I hate baby-sitting," said Floz. "You're just a pain, both of you. Get into bed. At once."

"Shan't," said Ross. "Unless you play some games."

"I want a wee wee," said Lindsey.

"And I want a drink of water," said Ross.

"You'll get the back of my hand, that's what you'll get," said Floz.

"And I want something to eat," said Ross.

"O.K., I'll get you a drink," said Floz, "but get into bed. First of all."

They both went slowly back to bed, sniggering, hoping for some fun and games.

Floz went into the kitchen and found there was a little bit of whisky in the bottle. She poured out two glasses, added sugar, and then gave Ross and Lindsey one each. She then sang a song to them. Before she had finished, they'd both fallen asleep.

Floz tiptoed over to each bed, very carefully, and tucked them in.

She noticed some felt pens beside Lindsey's bed so she picked out one and checked on her hand that it was working. She rolled up the sleeves of Ross's pyjama jacket and wrote on his arm, in very big letters—

Man Utd Are Rubbish

Floz went back into the other room and tried to waken up Martin. This was quite difficult. She shook him and shook him, shouted in his ear, banged him on the arm. In the end she got a cup of cold water and poured it over his head.

"I've got to go now," said Floz. "They'll be back in about an hour, O.K.? Tell them I had to go."

"What? Where am I?" asked Martin.

"I'm going. You can have all the money," said Floz.

"What money? Where?"

"Oh God," said Floz. "Don't be so stupid. The baby-sitting money."

"Thanks," said Martin.

"Just keep it all. I think I owe you some money anyway. Buy yourself a dry shirt. 'Bye, I'm off home now . . ."

Floz got into her house the secret way, without Fergus hearing her. She then crept up the stairs to Bella's bedroom.

She took a long time taking off the fur coat, giving several strokes, very slowly, before unbuttoning it carefully. She was very sorry she had ever told anyone. It was a mistake, she said to herself. She hadn't meant to.

Immediately the coat was off, she had changed back into little Flossie, ten years old.

She closed Bella's door and went into her own bedroom. Then she went out again. She had forgotten to brush her teeth.

"Yucky taste," said Flossie. "Don't want anyone to think I've been drinking any of those disgusting drinks. Imagine having no Ribena in that whole house. I thought they always left out nice drinks for baby-sitters. They're definitely on my Black List."

Flossie went into her bedroom, put on her pyjamas and got into bed.

"I'm not going baby-sitting any more. I've retired."

She noticed that her bedroom was still very untidy, just as she had left it after she had been playing with Ross. She told herself she would clear it all up in the morning, nice and tidy, the way her mother liked it to be.

Flossie pulled up the blankets so that only the tip of her little nose was sticking out.

"I don't think I want to be eighteen again. Well, not for a very long time . . ."

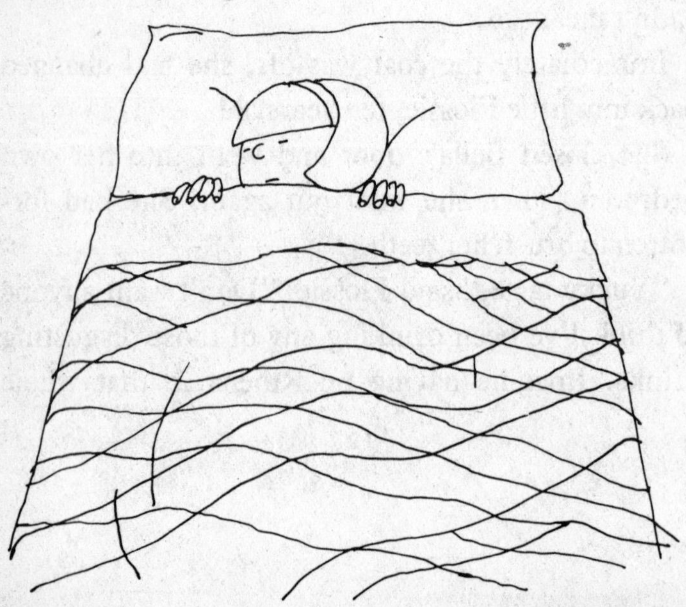